Classic Short Stories About Women –

by Rabindranath Tagore

translated from the original Bengali by

Suparna Chakraborti

Classic Short Stories About Women – by

Rabindranath Tagore

translated from the original Bengali by

Suparna Chakraborti

Subha

When the child was named Subhashini - *girl with beautiful speech* - nobody imagined that she would be mute. Her two older sisters were named Sukeshini – *girl with beautiful hair* - and Suhashini - *girl with beautiful laughter*. In consonance with their names, the girl's father had named his youngest daughter Subhashini. Now everyone called her Subha for short.

The two older girls had been married off with the proper inquiry and expense. Now the youngest remained as a silent weight on her parents' hearts.

Since Subha could not speak, most people believed that she could not understand, and they expressed doubts about her future in her presence. From her earliest childhood, Subha had known that her birth in her parents' household was a curse from God. As a result, she kept herself hidden away and tried to avoid being seen. She thought it would be a relief if everyone forgot her. Unfortunately, no person can forget his pain. Subha was always present in her parents' thoughts.

Her mother in particular saw Subha as a punishment for some shortcoming of her own. A mother

1

feels that her daughter is an extension of herself – more so than a son – and a deficiency in a daughter is a matter of personal shame. The girl's father, Banikantha, on the other hand, loved Subha more than he loved his other daughters; her mother - who gave her birth - saw in Subha some defect in herself and was frequently irritated by her presence.

Subha did not have the power of speech, but she did have two large black long-lashed eyes – and the slightest thought or feeling made her lips tremble like tender young leaves.

When we express our feelings in words, we must make a conscious effort. It is, in a sense, a process of translation. But black eyes don't need to translate; the mind casts its shadow unconsciously on the eyes, and feelings and thoughts ebb and flow at will. Sometimes the eyes burn with intensity; at other times their light grows dim; sometimes their gaze is steady and unblinking, like the moon when it sets; sometimes their glance darts rapidly from here to there like restless lightning. In those who have had no other language from birth, the language of the eyes is inexpressibly free and unfathomably deep – like a clear, translucent sky or a field where shadows

2

battle. Such people have a sublime, desolate quality, an aura of vastness and solitude. The girls and boys of the village were afraid of Subha for that reason, and they would not play with her. Her life was as lonely and silent as an empty afternoon.

∞∞ Two ∞∞

Subha lived with her parents in the village of Chandipur. A small river flowed past the village, typical of countless other rivers in Bengal. Personified, such a river would be the young girl of the household. The river was not wide; slim and diligent, it stayed within its banks and went about its work. Every person who lived near it had some connection with the river. There were villages and tree-shaded forests on both banks. Like a village goddess, forgetful of herself, the stream moved with rapid steps beneath the trees, cheerfully doing her beneficent work.

Banikantha's house was on the riverbank. His bamboo-fence, thatched house, cowshed, husking-room, straw-stack, tamarind trees, and groves of mango, jackfruit, and banana were within plain view of the canoe-bearing stream. I don't know how often the existence of the mute girl was remembered in the midst of this domestic abundance; but, whenever she had a moment of respite from her household tasks, Subha went and sat beside the river.

At those times, it seemed that Nature filled the void of Subha's silence. Nature spoke for her. The trickling water, the people's voices, the singing of the boatmen, the birdcalls, and the murmuring trees mingled with the bustle and the motion all around and broke like ocean-waves against the shore of the girl's ever-silent heart. The various sounds and motions of Nature are a kind of language without words, a universal variation of the language of Subha's large, black eyes. From the insects chirping in the undergrowth, to the silent heavens above, the world is filled with signs and gestures, singing, crying, and sighs.

In the afternoons, when the fishermen and boatmen went home to eat, when the villagers lay down to sleep, when the birds stopped singing and the ferry-boats and canoes no longer floated by, it seemed that the bustling world had suddenly stopped short with its work half-finished and turned into a terribly desolate place. Under the immense, burning sky, mute Nature and a mute young girl silently faced one another – one from the vast, sunny expanse and the other from a small patch of shade beneath the trees.

Subha did have a few intimate friends. Two cows named Sarbashi and Panguli lived in the cowshed. They had never heard Subha speak their names, but they recognized her footstep. Subha did make a characteristic soft sound, and the two cows understood its meaning more easily than they understood words. They understood – better than people did – when Subha was being affectionate, when she was scolding, and when she was asking for something.

Going into the cowshed, Subha would put her arms around Sarbashi's neck and rub her cheek against the cow's ear. Panguli would gaze at her affectionately and put out a tongue to lick her. The girl went regularly into the cowshed three times each day; and, she went in at other times as well. When she heard harsh words in the house, Subha would go to her two dumb friends – they guessed something of her pain from her patient, sorrowful look; and, standing close to her, they would rub their horns against her and try to console her with silent sympathy.

Besides these two, there were a young goat and a kitten who were devoted to Subha, although with them she did not have a friendship among equals. Day or night, the kitten unashamedly sought Subha's warm lap and prepared to fall blissfully asleep; he even hinted that he would sleep more comfortably if Subha stroked his neck and back with soft fingers.

∞∞ Three ∞∞

Subha had one friend among the highest class of beings. It would be difficult to describe the exact nature of their relationship, since this friend was able to speak; he and Subha did not share a common language.

Pratap was the Goswamy's youngest son. The man never did any work. His parents had given up hoping that he would apply himself and help support the family. Lazy people have one thing in their favor; they irritate their relatives, but they often become popular with other people. Since they are never occupied with work, they become common property. Cities need a few public parks that are free of domestic influence; similarly, villages need one or two unoccupied people who belong in the public domain. In times of leisure, for odd jobs and amusements, whenever an extra person is needed, these people are available.

Pratap's main interest in life was fishing. A person who is fishing can occupy a great deal of time with very little effort. Most afternoons, Pratap could be seen sitting by the river engaged in this activity. There, he frequently encountered Subha. No matter what he was doing, Pratap was always happy to have a companion. A silent companion is best for fishing, so Pratap understood Subha's worth. Everyone else called Subha, "Subha," but Pratap shortened her name even further and affectionately called her "Su."

Subha sat beneath the tamarind trees, and Pratap sat on the ground nearby with his pole, gazing at the water. Pratap liked to chew one *betel* leaf each day, and Subha prepared it herself and brought it for him from home. – I believe that as she sat looking on, Subha wished she could do some important work, that she could help Pratap in some way and somehow show him that she was not an insignificant person. But there was nothing for her to do. She prayed that God would give her extraordinary strength – she wanted to perform some feat that would astonish Pratap and make him say, "I never knew our Subhi could do that!"

If Subha had been a water-goddess, she could have emerged slowly from the water and left a jewel at the water's edge. If she did that, Pratap would stop his paltry fishing; he would pick up the jewel and dive into the water. When he reached the underworld, he would find – sitting in a silver palace on a golden divan – who else? – Banikantha's mute daughter Su – our Su would be a princess in that rich, silent underwater kingdom. Could it never happen? Was it so impossible? Actually, nothing is impossible – but, nevertheless, Su had not been born into a royal family in an underwater realm; she had been born into Banikantha's family, and no matter what she did, she could not astonish the Goswamy's son Pratap.

∞∞ Four ∞∞

Subha grew older. She began to know herself. It was as if –on a moonlit night – the tide of some unknown ocean had touched her soul and filled her with a new, ineffable consciousness. She saw, and considered, and questioned herself, but she could not understand.

Sometimes, on still moonlit nights, Subha opened the door of her bedroom and fearfully looked outside. She saw the full moon, alone, like herself, looking down on the sleeping world, filling the endless desolation. The moon throbbed with the mystery of youth – with delight and despair – but it could not say one word. A silent, anxious girl stood at one end of this silent anxious world.

Subha's parents grew more and more worried, burdened by their unmarried daughter. People had begun to talk. Some wanted to outcaste the family. Banikantha was a wealthy man – he could afford to eat fish twice a day – so naturally he had enemies.

The husband and wife had a serious conversation. Banikantha left the village for a few days.

When he returned, he said, "Let's take a trip to Kolkata."

Preparations were made for the journey. Subha's heart grew heavy with tears, like a morning veiled by mist. For several days, she followed her parents about their work, in the manner of a dumb animal sensing some unseen danger. She gazed with wide eyes at her parents' faces, but they did not explain.

One afternoon, as he cast out his line, Pratap laughed and said, "So – Su - I heard they've found a husband for you. Are you going away to get married? See that you don't forget us!"

He turned back to his fishing.

A deer that is pierced to the heart looks at the hunter who has struck her and silently asks, "Why do I deserve this? What did I do?" Subha looked at Pratap in just that way; she did not sit under the tree any longer. Banikantha had finished his nap and was smoking in his bedroom. Subha sat down near his feet and began to cry. Banikantha tried to console her, but tears began to roll down his own dry cheeks.

Tomorrow they would travel to Kolkata. That evening, Subha went into the cowshed to say goodbye to her childhood friends; she fed them with her own hands, then put her arms around their necks and gazed at their faces with all the language she possessed – her tears overflowed.

The moon that night was two days from full. Subha left her bed and threw herself down on the grass in her usual place beneath the trees. She wanted to clasp the earth – the silent, immense mother of all men – with both arms and say, "Don't let me go, Mother. Hold me in your arms and keep me here!"

One day, in their lodgings in Kolkata, Subha's mother dressed her daughter carefully. She twisted up Subha's hair and put gold and silver ribbons around it. As far as she could, she extinguished Subha's natural beauty, concealing it with ornaments. Subha could not hold back her tears. Her mother scolded her sharply, since swollen eyes would spoil her appearance, but Subha's tears would not heed the reprimand.

Subha's future husband came with his friends to see his would-be bride – the bride's parents became agitated, anxious, and afraid, as if a god had arrived to choose – in person – the animal that would be sacrificed in his behalf. In the dressing room, the mother made her daughter cry twice as hard with her scolding, threats, and commands; then she sent the girl out to face her examiner. The examiner inspected the girl for some time and then pronounced his judgment, "Not bad."

Her tears – especially – told him the girl had a heart. He calculated that the heart which ached today at the impending separation from home and parents would be useful to himself tomorrow. The girl's tears increased her value as a pearl increase the value of an oyster; they said nothing else in her behalf.

The wedding took place at an auspicious time; the mother and father returned to their home. Their caste status was preserved, and the future welfare of their souls was ensured.

Within a week, everyone realized that the new bride was mute. Nobody realized that she was not to blame. She had not deceived anyone. Her two eyes said it all, but nobody understood. She looked around in desperation, but she could not find language to explain; she did not see those familiar faces who understood her mute language.

The sound of unspoken, endless weeping echoed in the girl's eternally silent heart – only God heard that sound.

Subha's husband married again. This time, he used both eyes and ears in his examination and married a girl who was distinguished by her ready speech.

∞∞∞∞∞∞∞∞∞∞∞∞∞∞∞∞∞∞∞∞∞∞∞∞∞

The Skeleton

A human skeleton used to hang in the room beside our bedroom. At night, the breeze made the bones clatter and sway; during the day, we had to rattle the bones ourselves. At that time, we had a teacher who schooled us in classical literature and a student from the Campbell School who tutored us in osteology – the study of bones. Our guardian wanted us to be experts in several fields. Those who know us, know how far he succeeded; for those who don't know us, the subject is best not discussed.

Many years went by. The skeleton was removed from the room next-door, and osteology faded out of our minds; both disappeared without a trace.

Then, one night, we were short of beds for some reason, and I was sent to sleep in the room next-door. I couldn't fall asleep in the strange bed. I tossed back and forth and listened to the church clock strike the hours one after the other. The lamp in the corner gasped for breath for nearly five minutes before it died. At about that time, two or three deaths had occurred in the family. The struggles of the dying light naturally set me to thinking about death. It seemed to me that just as the light had flickered out and merged with the darkness, the small lights of individual human lives flickered out – some at night, some during the day – and were forgotten.

After a while, I remembered the skeleton. I lay in bed and imagined what its life had been like. Suddenly, I sensed that a living being was walking around and around the dark room, groping against the walls and brushing past the mosquito-netting around my bed. I could hear it breathing. It seemed to be pacing back and forth, searching for something without success. I realized that the apparition must be the creation of my own overheated brain; the sound of its footsteps must actually be the blood pounding in my own head. Even so, I shuddered. To dispel my baseless fear, I called out loudly, "Who's there?"

The footsteps approached my bed and stopped. A voice replied, "It's me – I'm looking for my old skeleton."

I decided that it should be easy to frighten away a figment of my own imagination. I clasped my pillow tightly, and said in a casual, familiar tone, "What a thing to do in the middle of the night. Why do you need to see that old skeleton anyway?"

The answer came back from the darkness close beside my bed. "What do you mean? My heart once beat inside those ribs! I lived twenty-six years within that frame – is it so strange that I should want to see it?"

"That makes sense," I replied at once. "Well, you go look for it. I'll try to get some sleep."

"Are you alone?" the voice asked. "Then I'll stay for a while. We can sit and talk. Thirty-five years ago, I used to be a living person who sat and gossiped with other living people. I've been blowing around the cremation-ground like a howling wind these thirty-five years. Tonight I'll sit here with you and speak like a human being once more."

Through the mosquito-netting I sensed that the spirit sat down beside my bed. Seeing that I had no choice, I said with some enthusiasm, "Very good! Tell me a story that will cheer me up."

"I will tell you the most entertaining story I know," the voice replied, "the story of my life."

The clock in the church struck two o'clock.

"When I was alive and still a child, there was one person I feared like the devil. He was my husband. He made me feel like a fish caught on a hook. I felt that a complete stranger had snared me, pulled me out of the sweet, familiar waters of my childhood, and carried me away – no matter how I struggled, I could not escape him. Two months after my marriage my husband died. My relatives lamented my misfortune. My father-in-law considered various omens and said, "According to the scriptures, that girl is cursed – like poison. I remember his words clearly. – Are you listening? How do you like my story so far?"

"I like it," I said, "It begins well."

"Then listen. To my great joy, I was sent back to my brother's house. The years passed, and I grew older. People tried to hide it from me, but I knew that I was extraordinarily beautiful. – What do you think?"

"It's possible. But I've never seen you."

"You've never seen me? What about my old skeleton?" The spirit giggled. "I'm only teasing. How can I make you see me – those gaping eye-holes once held large, lustrous black eyes, and the soft, smiling red lips I once had can't be compared to those hideous, grinning rows of bare teeth. When I think of how much soft, full, youthful beauty that dry heap of bones once carried – how my grace and beauty blossomed afresh day after day – I

16

want to laugh, and then I feel angry. In my day, the greatest doctor would not have believed that my bones could be used to teach osteology. One doctor, I know, told his best friend that I was a golden flower. He meant that other people's bodies might be used as specimens for osteology or anatomy, but my body was the pure embodiment of beauty. Does a beautiful golden blossom have a skeleton inside it?

I could feel that my every motion sparkled with loveliness and grace, like light sparkling on the facets of a diamond. I used to sit and gaze at my own two hands – I had hands that could conquer and break all the proud, arrogant manhood in the world. Subhadra, who drove away - proud and victorious - with Arjun in her chariot, must have had such fine and shapely hands, such soft delicate palms and lovely slender fingers.

My plain, bare skeleton lied to you, and I had to stand helplessly by, unable to speak for myself. That's why I'm more annoyed with you than with anyone else! Just once, I want to stand before you in that beautiful, blushing sixteen year-old form. You wouldn't be able to sleep for weeks – you would forget all the osteology you ever knew!"

"I swear to you," I said, "I've forgotten that already. And you've painted a brilliant picture of your bewitching beauty on the dark canvas of this night. You don't have to say another word."

"I had no female companions or friends. My older brother had determined that he would not marry, so I had no sister-in-law. I was alone in the house. I used to sit under a tree in the garden and dream. I imagined that all the world was in love with me – that the stars came out to gaze at me – that the breeze found excuses to sweep past me and sigh. I thought – if the pile of grass under my feet was conscious – it would become unconscious again at my touch. I imagined that the blades of grass were – in reality – all the young men in the world. They had transformed themselves so that they might touch my feet. For some unfathomable reason, my heart ached, and I was unhappy.

When my brother's friend, Shoshi-shekhar, graduated from medical school, he became our family doctor. I had seen him many times, through cracks in the doors and windows, when he came to visit my brother. My brother was a strange man – he never really opened his eyes and looked at the world. The world was not simple enough for him, and he tried to hide away in his own safe corner.

His one close friend was Shoshi-shekhar. Shoshi-shekhar was the only man I saw who was outside my own family. When, in the evenings, I sat like an empress among the flowers and the trees, the entire male race seemed to take the form of Shoshi-shekhar and fall at my feet. – Are you listening? What do you think?"

I sighed. "I'm thinking I'd like to be born as Shoshi-shekhar."

"Listen to the whole story first."

"One rainy day I came down with a fever. The doctor came to see me. That was our first meeting.

I lay with my face turned to the window so that the rosy light of the setting sun would fall on my face and disguise my pallor. The doctor came into the room and glanced in my direction. I immediately put myself in his place and imagined what he must be seeing. On a delicate pillow, in the evening light, he would see a sweet, tired face, as soft as a flower. Unruly locks of hair fell over the forehead, and the large, lovely eyes were modestly averted; long lashes cast a soft shadow on the beautiful cheek.

The doctor said softy to my brother, "I must check her pulse." I took my fine, shapely hand out from under the covers and held it out to him. I glanced at my hand and thought, 'I should have worn my blue bangles.' I never saw a doctor hesitate so over taking a patient's pulse. He felt my pulse in a bewildered way, with trembling fingers; he detected the degree of my fever. I, too, felt how fast his heart was beating. – You don't believe me?"

I said, "Why shouldn't I believe you? People's hearts do beat fast on occasion."

"After one or two more illnesses, I found that the thousands of young men at my imaginary assemblies declined in number until only one remained. My world was nearly deserted. Only one doctor and one patient remained.

In the evenings, I would secretly put on a light-orange colored *sari* and carefully arrange my hair, tying garlands of sweet, white flowers around my head. Then I would go out into the garden, carrying a small mirror.

Why did I carry a mirror? Didn't I grow tired of gazing at myself? I did not – because I didn't gaze at myself. Although I was alone, I became two people. I looked at myself through the doctor's eyes. I was astonished. I fell in love. I became affectionate. Then, a sigh like a hollow wind would arise in the depths of my heart.

From that time on, I was never alone. When I walked, I looked down and observed the way my feet touched the ground. I wondered how our newly-graduated doctor liked my footsteps. In the afternoons, the sun beat down outside my window; the silence was broken by the occasional cry of a hawk in the distance; outside our garden wall, a toy-peddler cried out - 'Toys for sale! Bangles for sale!' I spread out a snowy white sheet and lay down. With pretended casualness, I stretched out my hand. I imagined that someone was looking at it; he picked it up in his own two hands; he kissed its blushing-pink palm and slowly put it down again. Shall I end the story here – what do you think?"

"It's not bad," I replied, "I admit that it's unfinished, but I can pass the time very pleasantly until morning thinking of an ending for your story."

"Yes – but your ending would be too serious. There wouldn't be any humor in it. Remember, the skeleton must make its grinning appearance.

Listen to the rest. As soon as he had established a reputation for himself, the doctor set up an office on the first floor of our house. I often asked him – in a joking way – about medicines and poisons and what could kill a person painlessly. The doctor would grow talkative when asked about his trade. Gradually, through such conversations, death became as familiar to me as the people in my own house. All the world seemed full of those two things – death and love.

My story is almost finished. There isn't much left to tell."

"That's all right," I said softly, "the night is almost over."

"After some time I noticed that the doctor was always preoccupied, and he seemed embarrassed in my presence. One evening, he dressed more carefully than usual, borrowed my brother's horses and carriage, and prepared to go out.

I couldn't bear the suspense, and I went to my brother. After beating around the bush for several minutes, I asked, "By the way, *Dada,* where is the doctor going with our carriage?"

My brother said summarily, "To die."

"No," I said, "where is he going really?"

Shedding a little more light on the matter, my brother replied, "To get married."

I said, "Is that so?" and laughed heartily.

I learned that the doctor would receive twelve thousand rupees in dowry-money for this marriage.

I didn't understand why the doctor should insult my confidence by keeping his marriage-plans secret from me. Did he think I would fall at his feet and say, 'I will die if you do this thing?' Men are impossible to understand. In all my life, I saw only one man, and that one was enough to teach me about all of mankind.

When the doctor returned from his rounds that evening, I laughed a great deal and said, "What is this I hear, Doctor-Babu? You're going to be married today?"

In face of my gaiety, the doctor became not only embarrassed but melancholy.

"Are you having any music?" I asked.

The doctor sighed and said, "Is a wedding really such a happy occasion?"

I laughed even more, for I had never heard such a thing, and said, "That won't do! You must have music, and you must have lights!"

I pestered my brother with suggestions until he began to make preparations for an outright festival.

I talked incessantly about how much fun it would be when the bride came home, and what I would say and do. "Doctor-Babu," I asked, "will you go around feeling the pulses of strange women even after you are married?'"

The spirit giggled. "It's impossible to look into a person's mind – especially if that person is a man – but I know that my words pierced the doctor's heart.

The marriage was to take place late at night. In the evening, the doctor and my brother sat up on the roof and drank wine. That was their usual custom. Slowly, the moon rose in the sky.

I approached the two, laughing, and said, "Doctor-Babu, have you forgotten? It's time for you to go!"

I should say something here. Before my brother and his friend sat down to their evening drink, I had slipped into the doctor's office, got some powder, and mixed it into the doctor's glass. The doctor had showed me which of his powders was lethal.

The doctor emptied his glass with one swallow. He gazed piteously at my face and said, in a voice that was choked with emotion, "All right, good-bye."

Flutes began to play. I dressed myself in a Benarasi *sari*. I took all of my jewelry out of the safe and put it on. I put vermillion powder in the parting of my hair, making the mark of a married woman. When I had finished, I spread a bed for myself in the garden.

The night was very beautiful. Moonlight streamed down and made everything visible. A soft breeze blew from the south, carrying away the weariness of the sleeping earth. The garden was full of the sweet smell of flowers.

When the music of flutes faded away into the distance, when the light of the moon grew dim, when the trees and the sky and the familiar house began to vanish in the darkness, I closed my eyes and laughed.

I had hoped that this last bewitching smile would be on my lips when I was found in the morning. I had hoped that I would be smiling still when I entered my bridal chamber in the realm of endless night. What happened to my bridal chamber? What happened to my bride-s attire? I heard a clattering sound within myself and woke to find three boys studying osteology with my bones! The place in my breast where my heart once throbbed – where it pulsed with pleasure and pain – where youth bloomed afresh each day – a schoolmaster was pointing to it with a cane and explaining the name of each bone. I could find no trace of the last smile that had blossomed on my lips.

"How do you like my story?"

"It's a very good story."

I heard the harsh cry of a crow outside. I asked, "Are you still there?" There was no reply. The light of the rising sun came into the room.

∞∞∞∞∞∞∞∞∞∞∞∞∞∞∞∞∞∞∞∞∞∞∞∞∞∞

The Postmaster

For his first assignment, the postmaster was sent to the village of Ulapur. The village was very small. There was an indigo-factory nearby, and the factory manager had worked to have a post office established in the village.

The postmaster was a city boy. He felt like a fish out of water in his new rural surroundings. His office was a dark, thatched room. Behind it was a small algae-covered pond, and all around was jungle. The factory workers never had a minute of leisure; and, in any case, they were not fit companions for an educated city boy.

Moreover, this boy from Kolkata did not know how to interact easily with people. When he went to a strange, unfamiliar place, he was either rude and arrogant or shy and embarrassed. For this reason, he did not mix with the local people. At the same time, he had little work to keep him occupied. Sometimes, he tried to write a poem or two. The theme of the poems was this: that it was sheer bliss to spend one's days gazing at the trembling leaves and the clouds in the sky. But – God knows – if a genie from an Arabian tale had suddenly torn down the trees, and, overnight, built a proper road; and, if rows of

27

buildings rose up and shut out the sky, then this half-dead city boy would have felt that he was born again.

The postmaster's salary was meager. He had to cook for himself, and an orphan girl from the village did his housework in exchange for her meals. The girl's name was Ratan. She was twelve or thirteen years old. She had no likely prospect of marriage.

In the evenings, when the steam rose in spirals from the cowsheds; when crickets chirped in the undergrowth; when the intoxicated troupe of singers at the edge of the village began to beat their drums and sing loudly; when a poet sitting alone on a dark verandah watching the quivering trees would feel a slight quiver in his own heart; the postmaster lit a small candle in a corner of the room and called out, "Ratan!"

Ratan had been sitting outside the door waiting for this summons, but she did not enter the room immediately. She replied, "What is it, *Babu,* what do you want?"

"What are you doing?"

"I was about to light the stove – I have to do the cooking."

28

"Forget the cooking for a minute – bring me my *hookah*."

Soon after – with cheeks puffed out and blowing on the *hookah* – Ratan would come into the room. Taking the *hookah* from her hand, the postmaster would suddenly ask, "Ratan, do you remember your mother?" Such a question required a long answer. Ratan remembered some things, and she had forgotten others. She had loved her father more than her mother, and she remembered a few things about her father. Clear as a picture in her mind were the memories of a few evenings, when her father had come home after work. As they talked, Ratan would slowly sit down on the ground near the postmaster's feet. She remembered that long ago, she had had a younger brother; once, on a rainy summer day, they had played beside a small pond and pretended to fish with broken tree-branches. Ratan remembered that scene more clearly than she remembered many more important events. Often, they talked about such things until it was quite. Then the postmaster would feel lazy, and he would not want to bother with cooking so late at night. There were usually some left-overs, and Ratan would quickly light the stove and warm a few *chapattis* – that was enough dinner for both of them.

On some evenings, sitting on a wooden office-stool in a corner of the large, thatched room, the postmaster would talk about his own family, about his older sister, mother, and younger brother – the family his heart ached for - alone in this foreign land. These thoughts were always in his mind, but he could not speak of his feelings to the workers in the indigo-factory; he did not find it strange that he should open his heart to a young, uneducated girl. At length, Ratan felt so close to the postmaster's family that she began to call them 'Sister" – "Brother" - and "Mother." She even created images of them in her mind.

One afternoon, during the monsoon, a soft, warm breeze was blowing through the cloudless sky. It was like the warm, caressing breath of the tired earth. The sun drew a certain odor from the wet trees and grass. A tenacious bird recited its sweet, redundant complaint over and over again to its afternoon audience. The postmaster was not busy – but the smooth, swaying of the rain-washed trees, and the sun-brightened heaps of clouds, remnants of the temporarily-vanquished monsoon, were truly something to see. The postmaster was looking at these things, and he was thinking – at times like this, I used to have my dear ones close to me – my dear loving family. He began to think that the bird was saying that very thing, over and over, in the shadowy stillness of the empty afternoon, the murmuring trees were saying it too. Nobody knows it – and they might not believe it – but insignificant, underpaid sub-postmasters in little villages often contemplate such things on long, still afternoons.

The postmaster sighed, and then he called out, "Ratan!"

Ratan was sprawled beneath a guava tree, eating green guavas; hearing her master call, she quickly came running. Gasping for breath, she asked, "*Dada-Babu*, did you call me?"

The postmaster said, "I am going to teach you to read." All that afternoon, they went over the alphabet, and within a few days they had mastered letter-combinations.

During the month of July, it rained constantly. Drains and canals and low areas overflowed with rainwater. Day and night, the only sounds to be heard were croaking frogs and falling rain. The streets of the village had become impassable – people went to market in canoes.

One day, it had been raining heavily since morning. The postmaster's little student had been waiting patiently near the door for some time. Not hearing the usual call, she slowly entered the room with her bag and books. She saw the postmaster, lying on his bed. Thinking that he was resting, she silently moved to leave the room. `Suddenly she heard, "Ratan!"

Ratan quickly turned back and said, "Were you sleeping, *Dada-Babu*?"

The postmaster said weakly, "I don't feel very well – put your hand on my forehead."

Alone in this dreary village, without friends, the ill young man wanted someone to look after him. He remembered the soft touch of his mother's hand on his hot forehead. Sick, in pain, and far from home, he longed to see his mother and sister sitting beside his bed. His wish was granted. Young Ratan ceased to be a little girl. In that moment, she took his mother's place; she called the doctor; she gave him his medicine; and, she sat up with him all night. She cooked special meals for him, and she asked him a hundred times, *"Dada-Babu, do you feel a little bit better?"*

Many days later, the postmaster, thin and weak, left his sickbed. He decided, "No more. I must be transferred from this place."

Released from her nursing duties, Ratan went back to her old place outside the door. But now nobody called her as before. She peeked in, sometimes, and saw the postmaster – with a preoccupied expression – sitting on the stool or lying on the bed. While Ratan was hoping to be called in, he was waiting impatiently for a reply to his letter. The girl sat on the ground outside the door and studied her old lessons, over and over. She was afraid that she would make a mistake with letter-combinations if she was called in suddenly and quizzed. Finally, after a week, the summons came. With a quaking heart, Ratan entered the room and asked, "Were you calling me, *Dada-Babu*."

The postmaster said, "Ratan, I am leaving tomorrow."

"Where are you going?"

"I am going home."

"When are you coming back?"

"I'm not coming back."

Ratan did not say another word, but the postmaster explained that he had written, asking for a transfer. His petition had been rejected, so he was quitting his job and going home. For a long time, the room stayed quiet. The candle flickered; and, in one corner, the rainwater leaked through the thatched roof and dripped onto an earthen plate.

After some time, Ratan slowly went into the kitchen to make *chapattis*. She did not work as quickly as usual; she had a great deal to think about. When the postmaster had finished eating, she asked him, "*Dada-Babu*, will you take me with you to your home?"

The postmaster laughed and said, "How could I do that?" He did not explain the reasons why he could not take her home.

All night – in her dreams and in waking – the girl heard the postmaster's laughing voice saying, "How could I do that?"

Rising early the next morning, the postmaster found that the water for his bath was ready and waiting. Being a boy from Kolkata, he did not bathe in the river as the villagers did. For some reason, Ratan had not been able to ask the postmaster when he would be leaving.

Late as it was, she had carried the water from the river the night before, in case he needed to bathe in the morning. The postmaster finished bathing, and then he called for Ratan. She entered the room silently and gazed at her master's face, waiting for his command. Her master said, "Ratan, I will tell the new postmaster to take care of you, just as I have done. You don't need to worry, just because I am leaving." There was no doubt that these words were affectionate and kindly meant, but who can fathom a woman's heart? Often, in the past, Ratan had silently endured her master's scolding, but she could not tolerate these soft words. She burst out crying and exclaimed, "No, no, you don't have to say anything to anyone. I don't want to work here!" The postmaster had never seen Ratan behave in that way, and he stared at her in surprise.

The new postmaster arrived. After explaining to him all the duties of the office, the old postmaster prepared to go. As he was leaving, he called to Ratan and said, "Ratan, I have never given you anything, so today – when I am leaving you – I want to give you a little something that will keep you for a few days."

Keeping only enough for traveling expenses, he took out of his pocket all the money that he had earned.

Then Ratan dropped down in the dust, and, twining her arms around his legs, said, "I beg you, *Dada-Babu.* I beg you – you don't have to give me anything. I beg you – you don't have to worry about me –" She darted away.

The ex-postmaster sighed. Then, picking up his carpet bag and umbrella, and giving his blue-and-white striped trunk to the porter, he set out for the river.

When he had climbed into the boat, and the boat had left the bank; when all around him the river shimmered, like the overflowing tears of the earth, the postmaster felt a sharp pain in his heart – he saw the piteous face of a young village girl, and the familiar face expressed a deep, unspoken pain. He thought, "Let me go back. Let me find that friendless, orphan girl and bring her with me." But, the swollen river was flowing swiftly, and the sails were filled with wind. By that time, they had floated past the village; and, on one bank of the river, the postmaster could see the cremation-ground.

Floating on the river, the dispirited traveler suddenly realized a fundamental truth: in life there were many such partings; there were many deaths. It was no use to go back. No person belonged to any other in this world.

But, Ratan did not realize any fundamental truth. She wandered around and around the postmaster's house, weeping. She had a small hope that *Dada-Babu* might return – held captive by that hope, she could not leave. Poor, foolish human heart! The heart holds fast to illusion and seldom listens to the dictates of reason. Disregarding the strongest evidence, it clings tightly to false hope – then, in the end, it must cut the cord of attachment and run away, bleeding. When the heart finally does understand the truth – it is eager to be deluded again.

∞∞∞∞∞∞∞∞∞∞∞∞∞∞∞∞∞∞∞∞∞∞∞∞∞∞

In the End

Apurva-krishna had finished his B.A. degree and he was journeying home from Kolkata.

He was traveling down a small river. When the rains ended, the river nearly disappeared. Now, during the month of August, the water had risen to touch the village fences and kiss the fringes of the bamboo-thickets.

After days of constant rain, the clouds had finally dispersed, and the sun shone down.

If we could look into the mind of Apurva-krishna, sitting in a boat on the river, we would find that the river of the young man's soul also overflowed its banks and sparkled and shimmered with light.

The boat came to rest at the village landing. From the riverbank, through the trees, Apurva could see the brick roof of his mother's house. Apurva's family had not been told of his arrival, so nobody had come to meet him. The boatman moved to pick up his bag, but Apurva stopped him. Picking up the bag himself, he quickly and joyously stepped out of the boat.

The riverbank was slippery, and Apurva lost his footing as he stepped down; he fell in the mud, bag and all. He had no sooner fallen than peals of sweet, fluid laughter burst forth and startled the birds in a fig-tree nearby.

Apurva was embarrassed but he quickly recovered himself and looked around. He saw that a pile of new bricks had been unloaded from a merchant's boat. A girl was sitting on top of the heap, laughing so hard that she seemed in danger of going to pieces any second.

Apurva recognized her – her name was Mrinmoyi, and she was the daughter of their new neighbors. Their family had lived beside the big river far away. They had left their home two or three years before, when the riverbank collapsed, and they had moved to this village.

The girl's shocking behavior was often discussed. The men of the village affectionately called, her, "Crazy,' but the woman were perpetually alarmed, upset, and dismayed by her wayward nature. The boys of the village were her playmates; there was no end to her scorn for the girls her own age. In the world of the village children, this girl was the equivalent of a small cavalry.

Mrinmoyi was the apple of her father's eye, so she could afford to indulge in such reckless behavior. Mrinmoyi's mother often complained about her husband's indulgence, but she knew how much he loved his daughter, and how much it hurt him to see her in tears. Thinking of her husband – who was far away in another village – Mrinmoyi's mother could not bring herself to scold her daughter and make her cry.

Mrinmoyi's complexion was dark, and her short, curly hair just reached her shoulders. Her face was boyish. Her large, black eyes expressed neither shame, nor modesty, nor fear. Mrinmoyi was tall and strong and robust, but the villagers never thought to ask her age. If they had done so - they would have criticized her parents for letting her remain unmarried so long.

On the days when the landlord's boat swept up the dock, the villagers became flustered and agitated. The women near the landing quickly covered their faces with the ends of their *saris*, but Mrinmoyi would come running with her curly hair flying, carrying a half-naked child in her arms. Like a young deer, raised in a country without hunters or danger, she would stand and stare curiously, without fear. Then she would return to the group of boys who were her companions and describe in great detail the actions and behavior of the newly-arrived personage.

Our Apurva had seen this free-spirited girl a few times before, when he had come home on vacations. He had thought about her in his spare time, and at other times as well. We notice many faces, but one or two among them captivate us for no apparent reason. They captivate us not by their beauty, but by some other quality – perhaps by their lucidity. Most faces do not reveal the soul within, but in one face out of thousands the human soul manifests itself freely; such faces imprint themselves instantly on our minds. A restless, untamed feminine spirit shone in the face and eyes of Mrinmoyi and played over her features like a swift forest deer. Once seen, her vibrant, animated expression was not easily forgotten.

It goes without saying that Mrinmoyi's laughter – sweet as it was – distressed the unfortunate Apurva. Red-faced and embarrassed, he quickly handed his bag to the boatman and hurried away towards home.

The setting was lovely: the riverbank, the shady trees, the birds singing, the morning sunshine, the young man twenty years old. Of course, the pile of bricks was not worth mentioning, but the young creature who sat upon it lent a pleasant charm even to that hard seat. Only cruel fate could turn such poetry into farce with one small step.

Apurva walked home, keeping to the shade under the trees. He was followed by the sound of laughter that floated down from the mound of bricks. His clothes and bag were covered with mud.

Apurva's mother was delighted by the sudden arrival of her son. She immediately dispatched servants - near and far - in search of milk and cream and fish. Her agitation swept through the neighborhood.

When Apurva sat down to eat, his mother brought up the subject of marriage. Apurva was ready for her question. The subject of marriage had come up long before, but the boy had adopted the modern attitude and insisted that he would not marry until he had completed his B.A. degree. His mother had waited a long time for this day, so it was useless to make any further excuses. "Let's find a girl first," Apurva said, "and then we'll see."

"You don't need to worry about that," his mother said, "I've found a girl already."

Apurva was ready and willing to take that worry upon himself. "I won't get married until I see the girl

42

myself," he said. Apurva's mother thought that she had never heard anything so ridiculous, but she agreed to his request.

That night, when Apurva had blown out his light, he lay in his bed, alone and wakeful. Over the sounds and silences of the rainy night, he heard peals of high, sweet laughter. Over and over, he told himself that somehow he would have to atone for his fall that morning. The girl didn't know how knowledgeable he was – she didn't know that he had lived for years in Kolkata. Even if he had slipped and fallen in the mud, he was not some village boy who could be laughed at and ignored.

The next day Apurva went to see the girl his mother had selected. Her house was in their neighborhood, not far away. Apurva dressed with care. He exchanged his *dhoti* and shawl for a silk jacket and vest; and, he put on a round turban and a polished pair of shoes. He set out in the early morning, carrying a silk umbrella.

As soon as Apurva set foot in the house of his potential in-laws, he was showered with courtesies and attention. In due time, the frightened girl – dusted, polished, and painted – was led out before her future husband. She was dressed in a fine, colored *sari* and she had silver ribbon in her hair. She sat silently in a corner, her face almost touching her knees, and an old servant-woman sat behind her to give her support. The bride's young brother stared at the turban, watch-chain, and newly-grown beard of this stranger who was about to become a member of their family. Apurva twisted his mustache for a moment and then asked solemnly, "What do you study?" The bashful, swaddled figure in the corner did not reply. After two or three repetitions of his question and several pinches from the old woman, the girl murmured rapidly all in one breath – "Art – grammar – geography – arithmetic – and Indian history."

At just that moment, a restless, thudding sound was heard outside, and the next instant, Mrinmoyi burst into the room, hair flying and gasping for breath. Without so much as a glance at Apurva-krishna, she grabbed the hand of Rakhal, the bride's brother, and tried to pull him out of the room. Rakhal was busy sharpening his powers of observation, and he did not want to go. The old servant berated Mrinmoyi sharply, being careful to modulate her voice. Apurva-krishna preserved his solemn and dignified demeanor and held his turbaned head even higher; he sat

44

twisting the watch-chain in his vest. Finally, seeing that her friend stubbornly refused to yield, Mrinmoyi gave him a resounding blow on the back. She ran forward, pulled the bride's *sari* away from her face, and darted out of the room. The servant began to grumble under her breath, and Rakhal laughed delightedly at seeing his sister so suddenly unveiled. He did not resent the blow he had received, since that kind of give and take went on between the two all the time. In fact, Mrinmoyi's hair had once reached hallway down her back; it was Rakhal who had come up behind her and snipped her locks with a pair of scissors. Mrinmoyi had wrested the scissors from his hand and mercilessly cut away her remaining hair. Her bunches of curls had fallen to the ground like clusters of round, black grapes. Such was the relationship between the two.

The silent examination did not continue for much longer. The plump young girl retired into the house with her servant. Apurva stood up and prepared to go, solemnly twisting his scanty mustache. When he reached the threshold, he found that his shiny new shoes were not where he had left them; even after a lengthy search, he could not discover their whereabouts.

Apurva's hosts were extremely embarrassed, and they loudly abused the guilty party. Seeing that he had no choice, Apurva borrowed a pair of old house slippers from the master of the house. Wearing these and his stylish jacket, trousers, and turban, he walked carefully along the muddy village road.

The path by the pond was deserted, and there Apurva heard again the billowing peals of laughter. It seemed as if a fun-loving forest goddess was hidden away along the trees; she had seen Apurva's incongruous slippers, and she had not been able to restrain her mirth.

Disconcerted, Apurva stopped short and looked around. An unrepentant young sinner darted out of the thick undergrowth, dropped a pair of new shoes and turned to flee. Apurva quickly grasped by the arms and held her fast.

Mrinmoyi writhed and twisted, but she could not free herself from Apurva's grip. A beam of sunlight, coming through the trees, fell on the laughing, mischievous face, framed by curly hair. Apurva looked down at Mrinmoyi's upturned face, into her flashing eyes, much as a curious passerby might look down into a sparkling lucid stream and try to gauge its depths. He slowly loosened his grip and released his prisoner, leaving his task unfinished. If Apurva had been angry – if he had struck her – Mrinmoyi would not have been surprised. But, she did not understand the meaning of this silent punishment.

Laughter filled the air like the jingling bells of a restless dancer. Immersed in thought, Apurva-krishna slowly walked home.

∞∞ Three ∞∞

All the rest of that day, Apurva made excuses to himself and avoided going in to see his mother. He had an engagement to dine with friends, so he did not eat at home. It would be hard to say why a serious, educated, thoughtful man like Apurva was so eager to prove his worth to an insignificant, uneducated village girl – to make her fully aware of his inner greatness. What did it matter if a restless village tomboy thought he was an ordinary man? Why should he care if she laughed at him for a moment, then forgot his very existence and expressed such an earnest desire to play with an ignorant boy named Rakhal? Why did he want to tell her that he wrote articles of literary criticism for a magazine called *Vishvadeep?* Why did he want her to know that in his trunk - along with the cologne, the shoes, the camphor, the colored letter-paper, and the book called *Learn to Play the Harmonium* - was a notebook full of writing, waiting in the darkness for the coming dawn when it would be revealed to the world? The heart is illogical; and, whatever the reason, Mr. Apurva-krishna Roy, B.A., could not bear to admit that he had been bested by a simple village girl.

In the evening, Apurva went into his mother's room, and she asked him, "Well, Apu, how did it go? Did you like the girl?"

Apurva said hesitantly, "I liked one of the girls I saw."

"How many girls did you see?" his mother asked, surprised.

After some stammering and hesitation on Apurva's part, his mother finally understood that her son wanted to marry their neighbor Ishan's daughter, Mrinmoyi. So many years of education - and this was the boy's judgment!

Apurva was embarrassed at first, but his embarrassment faded when he heard his mother's violent objections. He stubbornly resolved, "I will not marry anyone else but Mrinmoyi." Marriage to that other doll-like girl seemed more and more distasteful to him.

After two or three days of argument, hurt feelings, missed meals, and sleepless nights, Apurva emerged victorious. Apurva's mother told herself that Mrinmoyi was still a child – that Mrinmoyi's mother had not raised her properly; after the wedding, the girl would be subject to her mother-in-law's control and her behavior would improve. In time, she even came to believe that Mrinmoyi had a lovely face. As soon as she thought this – however – the image of Mrinmoyi with her short, wild hair would come arise in her mind, and her heart would be filled with despair; but, perhaps if the girl's hair was tied back and properly oiled, even that defect might be remedied.

The neighbors all said that Apurva's choice was a brilliant choice indeed. Many people were fond of the 'crazy' Mrinmoyi, but, all the same, they did not think she would make a proper wife for their sons.

Mrinmoyi's father, Ishan Mazumdar, was notified in due time. He was a clerk for a steamer company. He worked in a small station by the river, where he sold tickets and supervised the loading and unloading of boats. He lived in a tiny house with a corrugated tin roof.

Ishan began to weep when he heard that Mrinmoyi had received a proposal of marriage. It would be hard to say whether his tears were born of joy or sorrow.

Ishan wrote to his boss in the company's head office, requesting leave to attend his daughter's wedding. The *sahib* deemed the occasion unimportant and denied the request. Ishan wrote home, asking that the wedding be postponed until the upcoming holidays, when he might have a week's vacation. But, Apurva's mother said, "This is an auspicious month, and I don't want to wait any longer."

Seeing that both his requests were denied, Ishan made no further objections. He continued weighing freight and selling tickets with a heavy heart.

Day and night, after that, Mrinmoyi's mother and the older women gave her advice about her impending marriage. They warned her not to be so fond of games, not to run or laugh loudly, not to talk to boys or eat too much – they soon convinced Mrinmoyi that marriage was a terrible thing. Mrinmoyi was anxious and afraid; she felt that she had been condemned to a lifelong imprisonment that would end with execution.

Mrinmoyi shook her head like a disobedient pony and insisted, "I won't get married!"

∞∞ Four ∞∞

Mrinmoyi was forced to get married, in spite of her objections.

After that, her lessons began. Overnight, Apurva's mother's house became her whole world.

The mother-in-law began the task of reforming the new bride. "Listen to me, Daughter," Apurva's mother said sternly. "You are not a small child. I will not tolerate such shameless behavior in my house."

Mrinmoyi misunderstand her mother-in-law's words. She thought that she must go somewhere else if Apurva's mother would not tolerate her behavior. That afternoon, they found that Mrinmoyi had disappeared. They began a frantic search. In the end, the traitorous Rakhal revealed her hiding-place. She was hiding beneath Radhakantha Thakur's broken-down cart beneath a *banyan* tree.

The reader can easily imagine the extent to which Mrinmoyi's mother-in-law, mother, and the do-gooders of the neighborhood criticized and disparaged her behavior.

In the evening, the sky became overcast, and rain began to fall. Apurva gently edged closer to Mrinmoyi in

51

their bed and whispered in her ear, "Mrinmoyi – don't you love me?"

"No!" Mrinmoyi exclaimed loudly, "I'll never love you!" Her amassed anger and resentment fell like a thunderbolt on Apurva's head.

"Why?" Apurva asked, offended. "What have I done to you?"

"Why did you marry me?" Mrinmoyi asked in reply.

It was difficult to find a satisfactory answer to that question. Apurva decided that one way or another he would subjugate that stubborn mind.

The next day, Apurva's mother noticed the signs of rebellion in her daughter-in-law, and she locked Mrinmoyi in her bedroom. At first, the girl paced back and forth from one end of the room to the other like a newly-caged bird. Then, finding no means of escape, she tore the bedsheet to pieces with her teeth. Throwing herself to the ground, Mrinmoyi wept and silently called out to her father.

Very slowly, someone sat down on the ground beside her. With a gentle hand, he tried to push her bedraggled hair back from her face. Mrinmoyi shook her

head violently and pushed the hand away. Apurva
brought his mouth close to her ear and whispered, "Come
on, I'll open the door. Let's escape into the back garden."

Mrinmoyi shook her head forcefully and said in a
loud, tearful voice, "No!"

Putting his hand under her chin, Apurva tried to lift
up her face. "Come and see who's here," he said. Rakhal
was standing near the door, staring helplessly at the
prostrate Mrinmoyi. Mrinmoyi pushed Apurva's hand
away without looking up. Apurva said, "Rakhal has come
to play with you. Won't you come and play?"

Mrinmoyi said, "No," in an irritated voice. Rakhal
left the room with a sigh of relief. He realized that it was
not a good time for a visit. Apurva did not say anything
more. Mrinmoyi cried until she fell asleep from
exhaustion. Apurva tiptoed out of the room, locking the
door behind him.

The next day Mrinmoyi received a letter from her
father. He lamented the fact that he had not been present
at his darling Mrinmoyi's wedding; and, he sent his
heartfelt blessings to the newly-married couple.

Mrinmoyi went to her mother-in-law and said, "I
want to go to my father." Apurva's mother was startled by

this impossible request and said, "God only knows where her father is, and she says, 'I want to go to my father!' What a strange idea!" She left the room without answering the girl's question.

Mrinmoyi went to her own room and closed the door. As a person might pray who has nearly lost faith, she said, "Father, please take me away. I have nobody here. I will die if I stay."

That night, when her husband had fallen asleep, Mrinmoyi slowly opened the door and left the house. Clouds occasionally obscured the moon, but there was enough light to see the road. Mrinmoyi did not know which road she should take to go to her father. She was guided by the belief that the road the mail-carriers followed led to every address in the world. Mrinmoyi began to walk along the path the mail-carriers followed. She waked until she grew tired, and the night was coming to an end. When a few birds began to flutter in the forest and doubtfully sing a few notes, Mrinmoyi arrived at the end of the road and saw a large marketplace beside the river. As she stood, trying to decide which way to go next, she heard a familiar, jingling sound. A breathless runner arrived on the scene, carrying a bag of mail over his shoulders. Mrinmoyi quickly approached him and said in a tired, pathetic voice, "I want to go to my father in Kushinagar. Won't you take me with you?"

"I don't know where Kushinagar is," the runner replied. He awakened he boatman in the mail-boat which was tied to the dock and floated away down the river. He had no time to offer sympathy or answer questions.

The dock and the marketplace gradually came to life. Mrinmoyi went down to the dock and called to the boatman, "*Mahji,* will you take me to Kushinagar?" Before the boatman could reply, a voice from the next boat said, "Who's that? Minu, my dear, how did you get here?"

Mrinmoyi replied with renewed earnestness, "Bonomali, I want to go to my father in Kushinagar. Will you take me in your boat?" Bonomali was a boatman from their own village; he was well-acquainted with this wayward girl. "You want to go to your father?" he said, "That's fine! Come, I'll take you." Mrinmoyi climbed into the boat.

The boatman untied the boat from the dock. The sky grew overcast, and a heavy rain began to fall. The swollen river rhythmically rocked the boat, and Mrinmoyi grew drowsy; she spread out the end of her *sari* and lay

55

down. The restless girl fell into a peaceful, childlike slumber, rocked to sleep by the rolling river.

Mrinmoyi awakened in her own bed in her mother-in-law's house. As soon as she was awake, the servant began to scold her. Apurva's mother was drawn to the scene by the servant's voice, and she began to berate her daughter-in-law harshly. Mrinmoyi stared at her mother-in-law with unblinking eyes. When Apurva's mother began to criticize the way Mrinmoyi's father had brought up his daughter, she went into the next room and locked the door.

Swallowing his embarrassment, Apurva went to his mother and said, "You know, it wouldn't hurt to send my wife home for a few days."

Apurva's mother upbraided him sharply for bringing this unmanageable girl – who made her blood boil – into their household, when he had had so many others to choose from.

∞∞ Five ∞∞

It rained and gushed all day, and the atmosphere indoors was equally stormy.

The next night, when the household was asleep, Apurva gently awakened his wife and asked, "Mrinmoyi, do you want to go visit your father?"

Mrinmoyi clasped Apurva's hand tightly and exclaimed, "Yes, I do!"

"Then come on," Apurva whispered, "The two of us can sneak away. I have a boat ready at the landing."

Mrinmoyi gave her husband a sincerely grateful look. She dressed quickly and prepared to go out. Apurva left a letter for his mother so she would not worry, and the two left the house.

As they walked along the lonely, village road in the dark, still night, Mrinmoyi felt a surge of confidence and trust in her husband, and she willingly took his hand for the first time. Her soft, confiding touch conveyed her sense of happiness and excitement, and her husband felt a tingling in his veins.

The boat left the landing while it was still dark. In spite of her excitement, Mrinmoyi soon fell asleep. The next day – what freedom and what happiness! They saw villages and market-places, mustard-fields and thickets; and they passed countless boats on the river. Mrinmoyi asked her husband a hundred questions about everything she saw - What was that boat carrying? Where were those people coming from? What was this place called? She asked things that were beyond the scope of Apurva's city wisdom, things that he had never encountered in his college textbooks. Apurva's friends would have been embarrassed if they had known that he answered every question, and his answers did not always correspond with the truth. He mistook sesame for linseed, and called Panchbere Rainagar, and he did not hesitate to confuse a *zamindar*'s court with an officer's court. Fortunately, these erroneous replies did not bother the questioner in the least.

The next evening their boat arrived in Kushinagar. Ishan Chandra was sitting in his small house. He sat, shirtless, on a stool pulled up to a small desk. He was writing in a large leather-bound account book by the light of a lantern. The newly-married couple suddenly burst into the room. Mrinmoyi cried out, "Father!" Such a word – spoken in such a tone – had never been uttered in that room before.

Ishan's tears overflowed. He could not decide what to do or say. His daughter and son-in-law seemed - to him - to be the crown prince and princess of some faraway kingdom. He wondered how he would find seats worthy of them among the bags of jute in his little house.

On top of that, there was the problem of food – that was something else to worry about. The poor clerk cooked his own meals, and he ate rice and lentils every day. What could he serve to his guests on this happy occasion? Mrinmoyi said, "Father, today we will all cook together." Apurva enthusiastically seconded her proposal.

There was not enough space or food in the house, and no servants. But, a fountain emerges with greater force the smaller the hole at its base – in like manner, Ishan's pinched face radiated happiness.

Three days passed by in this way. The steamer stopped at the dock regularly, twice a day; all day they were surrounded by crowds and noise; in the evenings, the riverbank was deserted, and then there was unlimited freedom. The three companions gathered their supplies; they mistook one thing for another and made mistakes, but somehow they managed to cook their meals. Then Mrinmoyi, with bracelets jingling, would serve their food with loving hands, and her father and husband would sit down to eat together. They laughed at the errors and omissions of the little housewife, and Mrinmoyi, who was

59

delighted, would pretend that she was offended. Finally, on the third day, Apurva said they must go home. Mrinmoyi plaintively asked to stay for a few days longer, but Ishan said, "No, dear."

When the time came to say goodbye, Ishan held his daughter close against his heart. He put a hand on her head and said, in a voice that was heavy with tears, "My dear, may you be the goddess who illuminates your husband's home. I pray that nobody ever finds fault with my Minu."

Weeping, Mrinmoyi departed with her husband. Ishan returned to his room, which was twice as lonely as before. There, day after day and month after month, he weighed freight and sold tickets.

∞∞ Six ∞∞

When the guilty pair returned home, they were greeted with stern silence. Apurva's mother said nothing about their behavior, and she gave them no occasion to offer explanations. Her unspoken accusations and silent reproach settled like a stone weight over the household.

At last, finding the situation intolerable, Apurva went to his mother and said, "Mother, the term will begin soon. I want to study law."

"And what will your wife do?" his mother asked, indifferently.

"My wife will stay here," Apurva replied

"That is not a good idea," his mother said, stiffly, "You take her with you."

"All right, I will," Apurva said, in an offended tone.

Preparations were made for the journey to Kolkata. On the night before their departure, Apurva found Mrinmoyi crying in their room.

Apurva felt as though he had received a sudden blow. He asked sadly, "Mrinmoyi, don't you want to go to Kolkata with me?"

Mrinmoyi said, "No."

"Don't you love me?" Apurva asked. He received no reply to this question. At times, this question has a simple reply; but, in other cases, this question is so complicated and involves so many things that a young girl really cannot answer it.

"Are you sorry that you will be leaving Rakhal?" Apurva asked.

Mrinmoyi answered simply, "Yes."

The learned, college-graduated young man felt a keen, acute envy of the boy Rakhal. "I won't be able to

come home for a long time," he said. Mrinmoyi had
nothing to say about that.

"I won't be home for two years or even longer."

"When you come back, bring a three-bladed knife
for Rakhal," Mrinmoyi said.

Apurva suddenly sat up in bed and asked, "You're
staying here, then?"

"Yes," Mrinmoyi said, "I want to stay with my
mother.'

"All right, stay here," Apurva said with a sigh. "I
won't come home until you write me a letter and ask me
to come back. Are you happy now?"

This question needed no reply, and Mrinmoyi
quickly fell asleep. Apurva did not sleep; he sat up in bed,
using his pillow as a backrest.

Late that night, the moon rose and moonlight
streamed across their bed. Apurva contemplated
Mrinmoyi in the moonlight. As he looked at her, he
fancied that she was a princess made unconscious by the
touch of a silver wand. If only he could find a golden
wand, he could awaken her sleeping soul and claim it. -
The silver wand was laughter, and the golden wand was
tears.

In the early morning, Apurva awakened Mrinmoyi and said, "It's time for me to go. Come, I will take you to your mother's house."

When Mrinmoyi stood up, Apurva took both her hands. "I have one thing to ask," he said. "You know I've done many things for you. Before I go – will you do one thing for me?"

"Yes," Mrinmoyi said, surprised.

"I want you to kiss me of your own free will."

Apurva's odd request and solemn expression made Mrinmoyi laugh. Restraining her laughter, she bought her lips close to Apurva's face and prepared to kiss him – but she couldn't do it. Mrinmoyi tried twice to kiss Apurva, and then, giving up the attempt, she covered her face with her *sari* and laughed. Apurva tweaked her ears in mock annoyance.

Apurva's was a difficult resolve. He felt that it was dishonorable to seize a thing by force, like a thief. He would only take what was freely given, like a deity graciously accepting a heartfelt offering. He would not extend his own hand.

Mrinmoyi did not laugh any more. Apurva walked with her along the empty road in the early morning light and left her at her mother's house. On returning home, he said to his mother, "I've thought it over, and I've decided that my studies will suffer if I take my wife to Kolkata. Besides that, she would be alone there, without friends. You don't want to keep her here, so I've left her at her mother's house."

Mother and son parted with deep resentment on both sides.

∞∞ Seven ∞∞

Mrinmoyi found that she could not settle down in her old home. The house seemed completely transformed. Time dragged slowly. Mrinmoyi had nothing to do, nowhere to go, and nobody to talk to.

The house and the village suddenly seemed empty and deserted. It was as if the sun had set in the middle of the afternoon. Today she wished - heart and soul - that she could go to Kolkata, and she wondered where this wish had been the night before. Yesterday she had been heartbroken at the thought of leaving the life she knew; she did not realize that her feelings for that life had changed. Mrinmoyi cast off that old existence with no trouble at all, as a tree sheds its withered old leaves.

Legends tell of sword-smiths who made swords so fine that a person could be cut in half with one and not know it until he moved. Nature's fine sword had severed Mrinmoyi's childhood from her youth without her knowledge; now, with this shock, her childhood fell away and only youth remained. Mrinmoyi looked on, surprised and hurt.

Her old bedroom in her mother's house no longer seemed to be her own. The girl who had lived there had suddenly disappeared. Mrinmoyi's heart and mind hovered around another house, another room, another bed.

Mrinmoyi was no longer seen around the village. Her laughter was no longer heard. Rakhal was afraid of her. He could not imagine playing with her now.

Mrinmoyi told her mother, "Take me home."

Apurva's mother was heartbroken, made miserable by the memory of her son's sorrowful expression when he left her. It hurt her to think that Apurva had left his wife with her mother in a fit of anger.

One day, as Apurva's mother sat thinking about these things, Mrinmoyi came in and touched her mother-in-law's feet; her pale face was covered by her *sari*.

Apurva's mother immediately took the girl in her arms; her eyes glistened. The two were reconciled in that moment. Apurva's mother was startled when she looked at her daughter-in-law's face. The old Mrinmoyi was gone. Such a drastic transformation is beyond the capabilities of most people; a change of such unusual magnitude requires unusual strength.

Apurva's mother had vowed that she would correct Mrinmoyi's faults, one by one. Before she could do so, an unseen teacher – using a simpler method – had bestowed a new existence on Mrinmoyi.

Apurva's mother understood Mrinmoyi, and Mrinmoyi understood her mother-in-law. They were united, as a tree is united with its branches.

Mrinmoyi was pained by the sweet, solemn, powerful sense of womanhood that filled every part of her body and mind. Just as the first clouds of the monsoon are heavy with rain, Mrinmoyi's first feeling was a tearful resentment. This feeling gave an added depth to her deep, lustrous eyes. "I didn't understand myself," she thought, "but why didn't you understand me? Why didn't you punish me? Why didn't you make me behave as you wished? When I behaved like a monster and wouldn't go with you to Kolkata, why didn't you force me to go? Why did you listen to me? Why did you obey my commands? Why did you tolerate my disobedience?"

Mrinmoyi remembered the day when Apurva had held her fast on the lonely road by the pond and looked into her eyes without saying a word. She remembered the pond, the path, the trees, the morning light, and, suddenly, she understood the meaning of that solemn, heartfelt look. She remembered how she had tried to kiss Apurva on the day that he left, and failed. Like a thirsty bird chasing a mirage in the desert, Mrinmoyi's heart flew back to that day, but no matter how hard it tried, it could not quench its thirst. Mrinmoyi began to think – if only I had done this at this moment – if only I had given that answer – if only such and such a thing had happened.

Apurva had been grieved to think, "Mrinmoyi doesn't really know me." Now Mrinmoyi wondered, "What does he think of me? Did he understand me?" She was ashamed to think that Apurva must consider her an ignorant, fickle, unthinking girl. She regretted that he did not know that she was a woman with a deeply loving heart. Mrinmoyi began to repay her debt in kisses and caresses, using Apurva's pillow as a proxy. Many days passed by in this way.

Apurva had said, "I won't come home until you write me a letter." Mrinmoyi remembered his words. She went into her room one day, locked the door, and sat down to write a letter. She took out the colored gilt-edged paper that Apurva had given her, and she began to think. Very carefully, making the lines crooked and the letters uneven, getting ink on her fingers and forgetting the greeting at the top, Mrinmoyi wrote, "Why don't you write to me? How are you, and please come home." She could think of nothing more to write – she had said all the important things. But, Mrinmoyi knew that people generally expressed their thoughts at greater length. She thought for a long time and added a few more lines – "Now you write to me, and write me how you are, and Mother is fine. Bishu and Punti are fine, and yesterday our black cow had a calf." With this bit of news, Mrinmoyi concluded her letter. She put the letter into an envelope and addressed it to Mr. Apurva-krishna Roy, bestowing a drop of sincere affection on each letter.

Mrinmoyi had no idea that she must write anything more than the name on the envelope. Afraid that her mother-in-law or someone else would find the letter, she gave it to a trusted servant to mail.

Needless to say, her letter did not bear fruit, and Apurva did not return.

∞∞ Eight ∞

The holidays came around but Apurva did not come home. Apurva's mother decided that her son must still be angry with her.

Mrinmoyi thought that Apurva was angry with her, and she was terribly ashamed of her letter. The letter was so insignificant – it didn't say anything at all. It didn't convey any of her real feelings. After reading that letter, Apurva would think that she was more childish than ever – he must despise her. Mrinmoyi's heart writhed when she thought of these things, as if it were pierced by an arrow. Mrinmoyi asked the servant over and over, "You did mail the letter, didn't you?"

The servant answered one hundred times, "Yes, yes, I put it in the mailbox with my own two hands. The master must have received it long ago.

Finally, one day, Apurva's mother summoned Mrinmoyi and said, "Daughter-in-law, Apu hasn't come home for a long time. I think we should go to Kolkata and

visit him. Will you come?" Mrinmoyi nodded her
agreement; then, going into her room, she locked the door
and threw herself down on the bed, clasping the pillow to
her breast and laughing and wriggling with happiness.
Gradually, she became calmer - then, anxious and afraid,
she began to cry.

Without informing Apurva, the two penitent
women traveled to Kolkata to obtain his forgiveness. They
stayed with Apurva's sister and her husband.

Apurva was despondent because he had not
received a letter from Mrinmoyi. That evening, he broke
his resolve and sat down to write a letter to her himself.
He could not find the words to suit him. Apurva wanted a
greeting that would express his love and his resentment at
the same time; not finding the proper words, he began to
feel disgusted with his mother-tongue. At just that
moment, a note arrived from his brother-in-law saying,
"Your mother is coming to Kolkata. She will be here soon,
and she will stay with us tonight. All is well." - In spite of
this last assurance, Apurva began to worry. He set out for
his sister's house without delay.

As soon as he saw his mother, Apurva asked,
'Mother, are you all well?"

His mother said, "Yes, we're all fine. You didn't come home for the holidays, so I've come myself to take you home."

"You didn't have to come all this way for that," Apurva said. "I've been studying for my law-exams." - Etc.

When they sat down to eat, Apurva's sister asked, "Brother, why didn't you bring your wife with you?"

Her brother replied solemnly, "I have to study." – Etc.

"What a fearsome man," said Apurva's brother-in-law. "It's a wonder he doesn't frighten little children."

They all laughed and joked, but Apurva was melancholy. He didn't enjoy their talk. He thought, "Mrinmoyi could easily have come to Kolkata if she had wanted to." His mother had probably tried to bring her along, but she had not agreed. Apurva was too bashful to ask his mother anything about it – human life and all the world began to seem like an illusion.

When they had finished their meal, a strong wind began to blow, and a heavy rain descended.

Apurva's sister said, "Brother, you must stay here tonight."

Her brother said, "No, I have to go home. I have work to do."

"What is so important that you have to do it tonight?" his brother-in-law said. "You don't need anyone's permission to sleep here one night. What are you worrying about?"

After much pleading and cajoling, Apurva reluctantly agreed to stay the night.

His sister said, "Brother, you look tired. Why don't you go to bed now?"

Apurva had been hoping to do just that. He wanted to be alone in his bed in the darkness, where he would not have to talk or answer questions.

Apurva found that his bedroom was dark. His sister said, "The wind must have blown out your light. Shall I bring you another light, Brother?"

"No, I don't need one," Apurva replied. "I don't keep a light burning when I sleep."

His sister left, and Apurva carefully felt his way to the bed in the darkness.

He was about to lie down, when, suddenly, a tender pair of arms embraced him tightly. Before he could exclaim in surprise, a soft pair of lips kissed him tearfully and passionately again and again. Apurva was startled at first. Then he realized that a long-held dream – which had been thwarted by laughter – was fulfilled today with tears.

∞∞∞∞∞∞∞∞∞∞∞∞∞∞∞∞∞∞∞∞∞∞∞∞∞∞

The Notebook

Uma had become a pest since she learned how to write. She wrote with coal on every wall in the house, "Water flows, leaves blow," in large, crooked letters.

Uma's sister-in-law had *Mysteries by Haridas* hidden under her pillow. Uma discovered her secret and wrote, "Black water, red flowers," with pencil on every page.

The dates and times in the family's new almanac were buried beneath Uma's sprawling letters.

Uma's older brother, Govindalal, was harmless to look at, but his articles were published regularly in the newspapers. From his conversation, his relatives and neighbors never would have guessed that he was a thinker. I honestly can't say that he ever thought about anything; nevertheless, he wrote, and his opinions agreed with those held by the majority of Bengali readers.

According to Govindalal, European science's view of the nature of the physical body was seriously flawed. Govindalal enthusiastically composed an essay on the subject. He employed no reason or logic and relied solely on the power of thrilling language, but the essay was delightful.

One quiet afternoon, Uma took her brother's pen and ink and wrote across the essay in large letters, "Gopal is a very good boy. He eats whatever he is given."

I don't believe that Uma intentionally compared the readers of Govindalal's essay with Gopal, who ate whatever he was given. Nevertheless, Uma's brother was furious. First, he slapped his sister, and then he took away her stub of pencil, her blunt, ink-smeared pen, and her tiny collection of carefully hoarded writing materials. Uma did not understand the reason behind her severe punishment. The hurt little girl sat in a corner and cried.

When his anger had cooled, Govindalal contritely returned to Uma the things he had confiscated. On top of that, he gave his sister a nicely-bound lined notebook to soothe her hurt feelings.

Uma was, at the time, seven years old. From that time on, the new notebook graced her lap during the day and resided beneath her pillow at night.

When Uma walked to the local girls' school – accompanied by a servant and with her hair tied back in a little braid – the notebook went with her. Some of Uma's classmates were surprised by her new possession, some were envious, and others were spiteful.

That first year, Uma carefully copied in her notebook, "The birds are all singing. Night is over." She sat on the floor of her bedroom, clasping the notebook tightly in her hands. Uma copied and recited loudly in a sing-song voice. She collected many verses of prose and poetry in this way.

The next year, bits of original writing began to appear in Uma's notebook. The writing was short and simple, with no introduction or conclusion. Here are a few examples.

In one place, the story of the tiger and the stork was copied over from Uma's reader. Beneath this was a line that cannot be found in any modern schoolbook or Bengali reader: "I love Joshi very much."

Don't imagine that I am writing a love-story. Joshi was not an eleven or twelve-year old boy. Joshi was a household servant of long standing, whose given name was Joshoda.

Uma's real feelings cannot be determined from the one line cited above. A conscientious historian would find the aforementioned declaration of love clearly contradicted two pages later in the same notebook.

Nor was this the only such case – Uma's writing was full of contradictions. On one page she had written, "I will never speak to Hari again." - Not Haricharan, but Haridasi – a school-friend. Not far from this were words which made it clear that Hari was Uma's dearest friend in all the world.

That same year, when the little girl was eight, the music of flutes was heard in the house one morning. It was Uma's wedding-day. The groom's name was Parimohan. He was a writer-acquaintance of Uma's brother, Govindalal. Although he was young and educated, Parimohan completely rejected modern ways. The people of the neighborhood praised and esteemed him for that reason. Govindalal tried to imitate his friend, but he was not entirely successful.

Weeping, her small face covered with the end of her Benarasi *sari*, Uma went to live in her father-in-law's house. Her mother had told her, "Child, mind what your mother-in-law tells you, help with the household work, and don't waste your time reading and writing.

Govindalal had said, "Be sure you don't write on the walls of their house. And don't scribble on Parimohan's essays!"

Their words made Uma afraid. She realized that there would be no forgiveness in her new home; through long years of reprimands and harsh words, she must learn what her new family considered faults and shortcomings and offences.

Flutes played that morning as Uma left home. But, I doubt that there was one person present in all that crowd who understood the feelings of the frightened little girl as she stood, trembling beneath her ornaments and Benarasi *sari*.

Joshi went with Uma to her husband's home. She would stay until Uma was accustomed to her new surroundings.

After much deliberation, the affectionate Joshi took Uma's notebook with her; the notebook was a part of Uma's childhood life; it would be a sweet memento of her brief stay in the home of her birth; the story of her parents' love was written on those pages in large, crooked letters. Having the notebook close by would give Uma a taste of girlish freedom in her prematurely-adopted role of housewife.

During those first few days in her new home, Uma didn't write anything at all. She didn't have time. Then Joshi went home.

That afternoon, Uma took the notebook out of its tin box and wrote, in tears, "Joshi has gone home. I want to go home, too, to Mother.

Nowadays, Uma didn't have time to copy passages from her schoolbooks – she didn't have the inclination either. Now there was no contradiction in Uma's writing. The next line in her notebook read: "If *Dada* comes and takes me home, I will never scribble on his essays again."

Uma's father frequently wanted to bring his daughter home for a visit, but Govindalal sided with Parimohan and opposed his wishes.

Govindalal said, "Uma should be learning to serve and obey her husband. We will be distracting her unnecessarily if we take her away from her husband and bring her here to her old home." Govindalal had mixed instruction and irony and written a beautiful essay on this very subject; his like-minded readers felt compelled to acknowledge that his words were absolute, irrefutable truth.

Uma heard about this essay and wrote in her notebook, "I beg you, *Dada*, please if you take me home just once, I will never make you angry again!"

One day, Uma closed the door of her room and sat down to write some meaningless, insignificant thing in her notebook. Uma's sister-in-law, Tilak-manjari, grew curious. She wondered what Uma did when she closed the door of her room. Tilak-manjari looked in through a crack in the door and saw that her sister-in-law was writing. She was stunned. No girl in their house had ever written in secret.

Tilak-manjari's younger sister, Kanak-manjari, came and looked through the crack as well.

The youngest sister, Ananga-manjari, stood on her tip-toes and looked through the crack with great difficulty; but, she, too, learned the secret of the closed door.

In the midst of her writing, Uma heard three familiar voices giggling outside her door. Uma realized what had happened, and she quickly put her notebook away in its tin box. She threw herself down on the bed in shame and fear.

Parimohan was concerned when he heard the news. If a girl began to study, she would begin to read books and plays, and then domestic life would be impossible.

Besides that, Parimohan had thought deeply about the matter, and he had discovered a profound truth. He often said, the holy power of marriage originated in the separate strengths of men and women. When a woman studied, her female strength was transformed into male strength. In the struggle between two male powers, the holy power of marriage would be destroyed, and the woman would become a widow. Nobody had been able to refute this statement.

That evening, Parimohan entered their room and scolded Uma sharply. He ridiculed her as well saying, "I had better order a turban so my wife can go to work with a pencil behind her ear."

Uma didn't understand the meaning of his words. She had never read Parimohan's essays, and she didn't understand that kind of humor. Uma cowered miserably in the face of her husband's jeering words. She thought she could never live down such shame.

Uma did not write for a long time after that. But, one winter morning, she heard a beggar-woman singing a song outside her window. The song told of the Goddess Uma, returning to visit her father's home. Winter mornings always awaken memories of childhood; when, on top of that, Uma heard the woman's song, she could not restrain herself.

Uma could not sing, but ever since she had learned to write, she copied down the words of songs and thus made up for her inability to make music. This morning a beggar-woman was singing:

They said to Uma's mother – Your lost star is returning.

Like a woman insane, the queen cried,-"Where? Where is my Uma, I say!"

Weeping, the queen cried, "If my Uma comes –

Come to me once, dear, come to me once.-

Come to me once – let me take you in my arms."

Two arms went round the mother's neck.

Her daughter asked – reproachfully – in tears, "Why didn't you come bring me home?"

Uma's heart was full of reproach, and her eyes filled with tears. In secret, she asked the singer to come into her room, and, closing the door, she began to copy the song into her notebook, misspelling most of the words.

Tilak-manjari, Kanak-manjari, and Ananga-manjari saw it all through the crack in the door. They clapped their hands and sang out, "Sister-in-law, we see what you are doing!"

Uma quickly opened the door and went out. "Please," she said, "please be dears and don't tell anyone. Please – I beg you – I won' do it again. I won't write anymore."

Uma saw that Tilak-manjari was looking intently at her notebook. She ran back and clasped the notebook to her chest. Her sisters-in-law tried to take it from her by force, but they could not do it. Ananga ran and summoned her brother to the scene.

Parimohan came in and sat down solemnly on the bed. In a deep voice he said, "Give me the notebook." When Uma did not obey, he lowered his voice a few notches further and ordered, "Give it here!"

The girl held the notebook tightly against her chest and looked at her husband with an unwavering, beseeching look. When she saw Parimohan rise to take the notebook from her by force, Uma dropped it on the floor. Covering her face with her hands, she sank down on the ground.

Parimohan picked up the notebook and began to read Uma's writing out loud at the top of his voice. Uma pressed herself against the floor more and more tightly. The audience of three little girls giggled.

Uma never saw her notebook again.

Parimohan had a notebook, full of sharp, subtle essays about fundamental truths; but, there was no righteous person strong enough to take it away from him and destroy it.

Alive and Dead

Sharada-shankar was the *zamindar* of Ranihat. His widowed sister-In-law, Kadambini, had no family of her own; her mother, father, sisters, and brothers had all died, one by one. She had neither husband nor children. Her nephew – Sharada-shankar's youngest son – was the pearl of her heart. After the child's birth, his mother had been ill for many months, and his widowed aunt had cared for him. When a person cares for a child which is not her own, her feeling for the child is stronger than a natural parent's feeling because she has no physical claim to the child. There is no societal tie between them, only the tie of love – love cannot prove its existence in society, and it does not want to prove itself. The uncertain heart loves its treasure the more intensely for its uncertainty.

The widow loved her nephew with all the pent-up affection of her soul – until, suddenly, one evening in July, Kadambini passed away. For some unknown reason, her heart stopped beating – all over the world, life and time flowed on, but that one, small, loving heart was stilled forever.

To avoid any discussion or inquiry, four Brahmin employees of the *zamindar* took the body away to be cremated immediately with little ceremony.

The cremation-ground was far from Ranihat. Beside it was a pond and a small hut, and a large banyan tree grew nearby. Miles of desolate fields surrounded the place. A river had once flowed past the cremation-ground, but its current was now completely dried up. The villagers had dug up a portion of the riverbed to make the pond. The local people considered the pond a worthy representative of the river that had once flowed there.

The four employees placed the corpse inside the hut and sat down to wait for wood to arrive for the funeral pyre. Time passed so slowly that two of the four, Nitai and Gurucharan, went off to investigate the reason for the delay. Bidhu and Bonomali remained in the hut to guard the dead body.

It was a dark, rainy night. The sky was filled with heavy clouds, and not one star was visible; the two men sat in the dark room without speaking. One of the two had matches and a candle tied up in a corner of his shirt; but, despite their efforts, the matches would not light – their lantern had gone out earlier.

They sat in silence for a long time until, finally, one man said, "Friend, I wish I had some tobacco right now. I was in such a hurry, I didn't bring any with me."

"I could go out and look for some," the other man replied.

Bidhu saw through Bonomali's attempt to escape. He said, "Really! And you expect me to sit here alone?"

They were silent again. Every five minutes that passed felt like an hour. They cursed the two who had gone to check on the wood. As the minutes passed, they grew more and more certain that Nitai and Gurucharan were sitting somewhere, talking comfortably and chewing tobacco.

Everything was perfectly still, except for the crickets and frogs in the pond, which croaked on and on. Suddenly, the two men felt the bed move slightly, and the dead body turned over.

Bidhu and Bonomali shivered and prayed silently. The silence was broken by a sigh. The next instant, Bidhu and Bonomali leaped up and raced out of the hut towards the village.

They had run nearly three miles when they saw their two companions returning with a lantern. They two really had been gossiping and chewing tobacco, and they knew nothing about the wood – still, they said, "We have men cutting down trees, and they will be here soon." Bidhu and Bonomali told their story. Nitai and Gurucharan laughed in disbelief and berated the two for leaving their post.

Without wasting any more time, all four returned to the cremation-ground. Going into the hut, they saw that the corpse had vanished – the bed was empty.

They looked at one another. Could a jackal have carried the body away? It seemed unlikely since they couldn't find even a scrap of clothing. They searched everywhere. On the wet, muddy ground outside the door of the hut, they saw the fresh, small footprints of a woman.

Sharada-shankar was not a simple man. It would do no good to tell him the ghost story. After much serious discussion, the four men decided to report that they had cremated the body.

When men arrived at dawn with wood, they were told that the job was already completed; there had been wood stacked inside the hut. They had no reason to doubt this story – a dead body is not so valuable that someone will want to steal it.

∞∞ Two ∞∞

Sometimes, when a body appears dead, its vital force is hidden away inside, and, given time, the seemingly lifeless person will recover. Kadambini was not dead – she had, for some reason, slipped into a comatose state.

When she recovered consciousness, Kadambini saw an impenetrable darkness all around. She sensed that she was not lying in her usual place. She called out once, "Sister!" – but in the darkness nobody answered. Frightened, Kadambini sat up, and she remembered the scene around her death-bed. She remembered the sudden pain near her heart, how breathing had become difficult. In a corner of the room, Kadambini's sister-in-law had been warming milk for the child over a fire. Unable to bear it any longer, Kadambini tossed wildly on the bed and cried out, "Sister, please, bring Baby once more. I feel so strange." Then everything grew dark – as if a bottle of ink had been emptied over a page of writing – and, in an instant, memory, knowledge, and consciousness were jumbled together. The widow could not recall whether she heard the child say "Aunt" one last time in his sweet,

89

affectionate voice; she did not know whether she had received this final, sweet farewell from the familiar world before she set out on her journey into the eternal, unknown realm of death.

At first Kadambini thought, "This must be hell – it is so dark and desolate." Here in hell there was nothing for her to see or hear or do; she must sit in this darkness forever.

Then a cool, wet breeze blew in through the open door, and the sound of croaking frogs came into the room. In a sudden rush of memory, Kadambini recalled all the rainy monsoon nights she had known in her short life, and she knew that she was still in the world. Lightning flashed and in a glance Kadambini saw the pond and the banyan tree, the desolate fields, and a small line of trees far away. She remembered that sometimes, on religious holidays, she had come and bathed in this pond. She also remembered how the sight of a dead body in the cremation-grounds had made her terrified of death.

Kadambini's first impulse was to go home, but she immediately thought, "I am no longer living. Why should I go home? That would bring misfortune on my family. I have been exiled from the world of the living – I have become a spirit."

If that wasn't the case – then how had she been transported, in the dead of night, from the safe interior of Sharada-shakar's house to this cremation-ground miles away? If her funeral rites had not yet been completed, then where were the people who should be here to perform those rites? Kadambini remembered the moment preceding her death in Sharada-shankar's comfortable house; now, finding herself alone in this dark, desolate, remote cremation-ground, she realized, "I no longer belong to human society – I have become something terrible – a doer of terrible deeds. I am a spirit."

As soon as Kadambini realized this, her old, earthly restraints seemed to fall away. She seemed to have unlimited strength and infinite freedom – she could go where she wished and do what she wanted. This novel feeling caused her to jump up like someone insane and rush out, like a sudden wind, into the dark cremation-ground – she felt no dread, or shame, or fear.

Kadambini walked until her feet grew weary and her body exhausted. The fields went on and on without end – some were rice-fields, and some were knee-deep in water. When the light of dawn came into the sky, a few birds began to sing in a bamboo grove near a village close by.

Then Kadambini was afraid. She did not know what new relationship she would have with the world and with living people. While she had been in the cremation-grounds and in the fields, as a part of the dark, rainy night, she had been unafraid; she had been in her own realm. People and the light of day seemed like terrible things to her now. People are afraid of ghosts, but ghosts were afraid of people as well; the two live on opposite sides of the river of death.

∞∞ Three ∞∞

After a night of insane activity, possessed by a strange mood, her clothes covered with mud, Kadambini looked so odd that people might actually have been afraid of her – village boys would probably have run away and then thrown stones at her. Fortunately, the first person to see her in this state was a gentleman.

He approached Kadambini and said, "My dear, you seem to be a respectable young woman. Why are you wandering here?"

Kadambini did not reply at first; she simply stared. She could think of nothing to say. It did not seem possible that she was still part of the world; that she looked like a young woman from a good family; that this gentleman was actually questioning her.

The gentleman said, "Come, my dear, let me take you home. Where do you live?"

Kadambini began to think. She could not return home, and she had no other family – she suddenly remembered a childhood friend.

Kadambini had not seen her friend Jogmaya for many years, since they were small children, but they still wrote letters to one another from time to time. They argued sometimes about which friend cared more for the other. Kadambini tried to prove that the greater affection was on her side. Jogmaya said – No – Kadambini did not possess even a fraction of her own feeling. Both were certain that if they ever managed to meet, they would be inseparable.

Kadambini told the gentleman, "I would like to go to Shripati Charan Babu's house in Nishindapur."

The gentleman was on his way to Kolkata. Nishindapur was some distance away, but he could arrange to pass through it on his way. The gentleman made the arrangements himself and escorted Kadambini to Shripati Charan Babu's house.

The two friends were reunited. They did not recognize one another at first; then each saw in the other the resemblance of her childhood friend.

Jogmaya said, "Oh dear! Can this be true? I never imagined that I would see you in person. But how did you manage to come? Did your husband's family actually give you permission?"

Kadambini was silent; finally she said, "Don't ask me about my husband's family. Let me be your servant – give me a corner. I will work in your house."

"My goodness!" Jogmaya replied. "How could I let you do that? Why should you be a servant? You're my friend, you're my..." - Etc.

Shripati suddenly entered the room. Kadambini looked at him steadily for a moment, then slowly left the room – she showed no signs of shame or embarrassment.

Jogmaya grew flustered and began to make excuses for her friend, in case her husband was offended. She had to say so little – and Shripati accepted her excuses so readily – that Jogmaya remained uneasy.

Kadambini had come to the house of her bosom friend, but she could not be close to Jogmaya – death was a barrier between them. Two people cannot be friends if one is always suspicious, and the other is always conscious of something she must conceal. Kadambini looked at Jogmaya and thought, "She – with her husband and household – lives far away in another world. With her affections and duties and attachments, she belongs to the world of living people, while I am an empty shadow. She lives in the physical world, while I live in the inner, spiritual world.

Jogmaya was also uneasy – she did not understand the situation. Women cannot tolerate mysteries – because one can write poems about mysteries, or struggle against them, or study them – but one cannot keep house with them. So, when a woman encounters a mystery, she either ignores its existence or she interprets it in her own way and turns it into something useful – if she can't do either one, then she becomes very angry with it.

The more incomprehensible Kadambini became, the more Jogmaya was angry with her; she thought, "Why should this burden fall on my shoulders?"

Another problem arose. Kadambini was afraid of herself. People who are afraid of ghosts, fear their own backsides as well – they are afraid of everything they cannot see. Kadambini's fear, on the other hand, was centered on herself; she feared nothing outside of herself.

Driven by her fear, Kadambini sometimes screamed out loud when she was alone in her room in the afternoons; in the evening, when candles were lit, she shivered at the sight of her own shadow.

Kadambini's feeling was contagious, and a sense of fear spread throughout the household. Jogmaya and the servants began to see ghosts as well.

The situation became so bad that – on one occasion – Kadambini left her room in the middle of the night and came crying to Jogmaya's door. "Sister, sister," she said, "I beg you, please, don't leave me alone."

Her words frightened Jogmaya, but they made her angry as well. She wanted to turn Kadambini out of the house that very instant.

Shripati calmed his wife with some difficulty and kindly gave Kadambini a place in the next room.

The next day, Shripati suddenly came into Jogmaya's room. Jogmaya began with unusual sharpness,

"Tell me – what sort of man are you? A woman leaves her home – she lives in your house for one month and shows no signs of leaving – and I don't hear one complaint from you? Tell me – what are you thinking? You men are all alike."

Men generally have an indiscriminate partiality for the weaker sex, and they are quick to find fault with them for that very reason. Shripati had sworn to Jogmaya that he did not feel more than a friendly amount of sympathy for the beautiful and helpless Kadambini, but his actions showed that he did feel more.

Shripati thought to himself, "Her in-laws must have abused the poor, childless widow. Unable to bear it any longer, Kadambini has sought shelter in my house. She has no father or mother, how can I turn her away?" Shripati was reluctant to investigate her story, and he did not want to hurt Kadambini by pressing her for unpleasant details.

Jogmaya began to criticize her husband's dormant sense of duty. Shripati realized that he must contact Kadambini's family if he wished to live in peace with his wife. In the end, he decided that a letter – out of the blue

—might not produce the best results. He determined to go to Ranihat himself and do what must be done.

Shripati left, and Jogmaya went to Kadambini and said, "Friend, you really shouldn't stay here much longer. What will people say?"

Kadambini gazed solemnly at Jogmaya and replied, "What do people have to do with me?"

Jogmaya was stunned by her words. Becoming angry, she said, "People may be nothing to you – but they are something to me. How can we keep a woman here who belongs to another household?"

"Where is my home?" Kadambini replied.

"Death take her," Jogmaya thought, "What is the unfortunate woman saying?"

"I am no relation to you," Kadambini said, slowly. "I don't belong in this world. You all laugh and cry and love. You have your own families, while I can only look on. You are living human beings, but I am only a shadow. I don't understand why God has kept me here among you in your world. You all are afraid that I will be a curse on your happy lives – and I don't understand my relation to any of you. But, since God has not given me another place, I must live near you, even though the difference between us will always be visible."

Kadambini's words and appearance were such that Jogmaya did understand something of what she said, although she did not understand the truth. She could make no reply, and she did not say anything more. Slowly and solemnly, Jogmaya left the room.

∞∞ **Four** ∞∞

It was nearly ten o'clock when Shripati returned from Ranihat. Torrents of rain flooded the earth. The constant sound of falling water made it seem that the rain and the night would never end.

"What happened?" Jogmaya said.

"It's a long story," Shripati replied. "I'll tell you later." He changed his clothes, ate his dinner, took a pinch of tobacco, and went to bed. He seemed very thoughtful.

Jogmaya had restrained her curiosity for a long time. As soon as she lay down, she said, "All right, tell me what happened."

"You must have made a mistake," Shripati replied.

This statement angered Jogmaya. Women never make mistakes; and, if they do, a prudent man doesn't

99

refer to them; he accepts the blame himself. Jogmaya said dryly, "What mistake was that?"

"The woman you have taken into your house is not your friend Kadambini."

A statement like that would make anyone angry – and if one's husband says such a thing, here is no question that one will be furious. "Are you telling me," Jogmaya said, "that I can't recognize my friend – I have to learn who she is from you?"

They must look at the evidence, Shripati explained. There was no doubt that Jogmaya's friend Kadambini had passed away.

"Listen to that!" Jogmaya said. "You must have goofed things up. You didn't go to the right place, or you didn't understand what they said. A simple letter would have made everything clear – who told you to go yourself?"

Shripati was annoyed by his wife's lack of confidence in his judgment. He recounted all the facts he had discovered, but to no avail. Husband and wife spent half the night arguing back and forth.

They both agreed that Kadambini should be turned out of the house immediately. Shripati believed that

Kadambini was an impostor who had deceived his wife, and Jogmaya believed that Kadambini was a woman who had deserted her family – but neither would accept defeat.

Their voices grew louder and louder, and both forgot that Kadambini was sleeping in the next room.

One said, "A nice mess this is! I tell you – I heard it with my own ears!"

The other said loudly, "So what? I saw her with my own eyes!"

In the end, Jogmaya asked, "All right, tell me, when did Kadambini die?"

She thought that she could produce a letter from Kadambini dated after her supposed death and prove that Shripati had made a mistake. Shripati named a date. The two calculated and discovered that the date in question was the day before Kadambini had arrived at their house. When she heard that, Jogmaya's heart skipped a beat, and Shripati began to feel uneasy.

Just then, the door of their room opened, and a damp breeze extinguished the light. The room was flooded with darkness in an instant. Kadambini came into the room. It was then the dead of night, and rain was falling heavily outside.

Kadambini said, "I am your friend Kadambini, but I am no longer alive. I am dead."

Jogmaya screamed in fright. Shripati was rendered speechless.

"I have died – but have I done anything to hurt you? If I have no place in the netherworld and no place here – then where am I to go?" In the darkness of the night, Kadambini cried out as if she would awaken the sleeping God, "Where am I to go?"

Leaving the husband and wife unconscious in the dark room, Kadambini went out into the wide world to find a place for herself.

∞∞ Five ∞∞

It is difficult to say how Kadambini made her way back to Ranihat. At first, she hid from everyone. She spent the day, without food, hiding in a broken-down temple.

When the light had faded from the early monsoon evening, and the villagers had sought shelter from the approaching storm, Kadambini left her hiding place. Her heart beat fast when she reached the threshold of her old home. She pulled the end of her *sari* far over her face; and, mistaking her for a servant, the doormen did not bar her from going in. The storm broke suddenly, and the wind began to blow in gusts.

At that moment, Sharada-shankar's wife was playing cards with her husband's widowed sister. The maidservant was in the kitchen, and Sharada-shankar's young son was sleeping in the bedroom; the boy was feverish. Kadambini slipped past the two women and entered the child's room. She herself did not know why she had returned to this house; she only knew that she wanted to see the child one last time. She did not consider what would happen or where she would go after that.

By candlelight, Kadambini saw the ill, emaciated child sleeping with clenched fists. At the sight of him, her tortured heart hungered for the boy, and she clasped him to her breast with all her strength. At the same time, Kadambini thought, "Without me here – who will look after this child? His mother likes company and gossip and games. I looked after him from the day he was born – she never had to worry about him. Who will look after him now with as much care as I did?"

Half-asleep, the boy rolled over and said, "Give me some water, Auntie."

"Dear child! You haven't forgotten your Auntie yet!" Kadambini quickly found a pitcher, and, sitting the child in her lap, gave him water.

While he was still half-asleep, the boy did not find it strange that his aunt should give him water, just as she had always done. Finally, when Kadambini had kissed him to her heart's content and put him back to bed, he sat up, embraced his aunt, and said, "Auntie, did you die?"

"Yes, child," his aunt replied.

"But you've come back to me! You won't die any more?"

Before Kadambini could answer, a commotion arose. The maid had come into the room, carrying a bowl of tapioca pudding. She suddenly dropped the bowl, exclaimed, "Dear God!" and fainted.

The mistress of the house heard her cry and came running. As soon as she entered the room, she became as stiff as a wooden statue; she could neither flee nor make a sound.

The commotion frightened the child. He began to cry and said, "You go now, Auntie."

Kadambini finally understood that she was not dead – the familiar house and everything belonging to it -

her little nephew - her love for him – all were still vibrantly alive. In Jogmaya's house, she had realized that her childhood friend was dead; in that room, she realized that her little nephew's aunt was still very much alive.

"Sister, why are you all afraid of me?" Kadambini asked plaintively. "You see – I am just the same as I was."

The mistress of the house could remain on her feet no longer – she fainted. Having been summoned by his sister, Sharada-shankar himself came into the room. With folded hands, he said to Kadambini, "Sister-in-law, is this right? Satish is the only male child in my family – why do you curse him? We are your family, after all. Since you died, the boy has wasted away, day by day. The fever never leaves him, and day and night, he cries out, 'Auntie - Auntie!' Since you have taken leave of this world, you must sever this tie – we will bless you for it."

Kadambini could not bear it any longer. She cried out wildly, "I am not dead – not dead! How can I make you understand that I didn't die? You see – I am alive!"

She picked up a metal bowl from the floor and struck her forehead with it. Blood spurted from the wound.

"You see – I am alive!" she repeated

105

Sharada-shankar remained standing like a statue; the frightened child called for his father; the two unconscious women lay on the floor where they had fallen.

"I am not dead – I am not dead – I am not dead!" Kadambini screamed. With a wail, she ran out of the room, down the stairs, and straight into the pond behind the house. In the room upstairs, Sharada-shankar heard a splash.

It rained all night and all morning, and the next afternoon it was still raining steadily. With her death, Kadambini proved that she had not died.

∞∞∞∞∞∞∞∞∞∞∞∞∞∞∞∞∞∞∞∞∞∞∞∞∞∞∞∞

Printed in Great Britain
by Amazon

80107098R00068